William Krause

Bianca

A play of three acts and two changes of scenes

William Krause

Bianca
A play of three acts and two changes of scenes

ISBN/EAN: 9783337107949

Printed in Europe, USA, Canada, Australia, Japan

Cover: Foto ©Andreas Hilbeck / pixelio.de

More available books at **www.hansebooks.com**

BIANCA.

A Play of Three Acts and Two Changes of Scenes.

ACTRESSES AND ACTORS.

MISS TECLA,
MISS BIANCA,
DR. GRAEFFE,
EDWIN, his Son,
ALFRED, Friend of EDWIN, and
  Brother of BIANCA.
STUDENTS, { WEBSTER, CLAY,
        { SUMNER, SCHURZ.

THE HONORABLE SENATOR
  SCHOENLEIN,
MRS. SENATOR SCHOENLEIN,
MISS GÜTIG, Aunt of BIANCA,
HERONIMUS LUCKY, Esq.,
A. EMSIG, Esq., a retired Millionaire,
JULIA, Maid Servant in the house
  of Senator SCHOENLEIN.

BY

WILLIAM E. F. KRAUSE,

AUTHOR OF VARIOUS POETICAL AND OTHER WORKS IN THE
ENGLISH AND GERMAN LANGUAGES.

SAN FRANCISCO:

PRINTED BY JOSEPH WINTERBURN & COMPANY.

417 Clay Street, between Battery and Sansome.

1872.

BIANCA.

A PLAY OF THREE ACTS AND TWO CHANGES OF SCENES.

The Scene of the first two Acts is located at Oakland, in Dr. Merritt's beautiful Garden, near the Lake.

The Scene of the third Act—A Drawing-Room at the Residence of the Hon. Senator Schoenlein, in Martinez.

THE ACTRESSES AND ACTORS.

MISS TECLA,
MISS BIANCA,
DR. GRAEFFE,
EDWIN, his Son,
ALFRED, Friend of Edwin, and Brother of Bianca.
Students, { WEBSTER, CLAY, SUMNER, SCHURZ.

THE HONORABLE SENATOR SCHOENLEIN,
MRS. SENATOR SCHOENLEIN,
MISS GÜTIG, Aunt of Bianca,
HERONIMUS LUCKY, Esq.,
A. EMSIG, Esq., a retired Millionaire,
JULIA, Maid Servant in the house of Senator Schoenlein.

THE FIRST ACT.

Almost immediately upon the somewhat elevated shores of Lake Merritt, which are here adorned with a number of weeping willows, at the time in their luxuriant light-green foliage—a romantic spot, where two young ladies of remarkable loveliness, who have ingeniously escaped their girlhood but upon the last ball of the preceding winter, as so handsomely arranged by Messieurs the Alumni, are busily engaged gathering nimophilas, and those sweet little rose-colored star-flowers which, in sisterhood with the so-called Maiden's Hair, are the pride of the Flora of California. At the same time these aforesaid charming young ladies converse together most happily as follows :

Tecla (a beautiful blonde, gently addressing her friend):—Bianca ! how you are lost in reverie !

Bianca (a lovely brunette, generally with extraordinary vivacity in her graceful manners — touched to the quick)—Oh, Tecla ! you frighten me !

TECLA (laughing)—Thou art born to be beloved.

BIANCA (quickly)—What a comprehensive consolation!

TECLA (changing color)—Alas! these charming flowers! they remind me of Krause's latest poem on Pacheco. How delightful it must be there, at this time of the year!

BIANCA (to herself, almost inaudibly, and very diligently gathering clarkias)—Only now, and now only, do I know that I love him—dearly, passionately love him. The most remarkable scenery, friends, flowers, in reality, everything, leaves me inanimate—completely so—without him!

TECLA (calmly)—Oh, do let us entreat of our parents to visit that beautiful city!

BIANCA (quickly looking up at Tecla)—Dear Tecla! pray excuse me—what did you say?

TECLA (calmly)—Well, simply, we shall visit Pacheco. My father never refuses me anything which I anxiously desire; and I shall beg of Mr. Waldsworth to telegraph at once.

BIANCA (gracefully rising, and in high glee)—Pacheco did you say? —you want to visit Pacheco? Alas! there I have often been. In those neighboring hills it is so beautiful! and in our own Martinez, where Edwin searched for sapphires. [Instantaneously embracing Tecla]—Do come—come as quickly as you can.

TECLA (kissing Bianca)—How sweet you are!

(The two young ladies take their bouquets, and, in the happiest mood imaginable, hasten away.

Breaking through the low-hanging-at-this-time-of-the-year, densely-leaved boughs of one of the aforementioned weeping willows, appears a gentleman in the prime of life, with the gun upon his arm. Deliberately advancing, he lays down the gun upon probably the identical spot which the young ladies had just left, and says):

DR. GRAEFFE (calmly and thoughtfully)—Edwin! Edwin! My Edwin has got exactly the same passion to look for sapphires, and as yet, unfortunately, not find any. Nevertheless, he is quite right—all the treasures of the globe are to be found in California. Only labor, perseverance, and moderation in everything, and everybody becomes rich. Strange! who can that lady have been? Such a voice! so melodious, sweet, and clear, like a silver bell. Perhaps a child; more likely, however, a diamond, which Edwin has overlooked while his eye was intently fixed upon detecting the beautiful dark violet-blue of the sapphire. [Pensively]—Oh, man! thou gatherest treasures— inanimate pebbles; but leavest unnoticed the ever-living and inspiring love.

(The Doctor **sits down, while** his eyes search for an unhindered view over the **blue** waters of the gently-rippled lake into the distant hills, passing **in** the direction **of** Mr. Newton's handsome bowery of happiness, in order to enjoy with unspeakable delight **the** panoramic view of **one** of the finest landscapes which Nature has ever bountifully designed **to please a** feeling heart.)

How grand ! **how superb** ! How happy should every one be who, in good health of **body** and soul, resides in California ! **What** more exalted wisdom than to comparatively acknowledge the **fact,** and to fully and gratefully appreciate it ! **A thousand** dollars **for a grand** picture of **this scene** by Wandesforde, **Campion or** Watkins! **And how** gladly would I **take a hundred shares in a steam-ship line which** should land the German immigrant **direct from Hamburg in San Francisco,** or *via* Aspinwall either, so **long as New York is avoided, which is** always kind enough to extend the hospitalities **of the city and** neighboring **villages** to immigrants an indefinite **length of time.**

(Suddenly rising, walks to and fro, and says):

Edwin—most **likely I shall cure him. No more is the glaucoma of the** eye a **dangerous defect than is the glaucoma of the soul ;** which latter **my** experience **of the world shall** fathom thoroughly. Sickness of **the** soul, provided the **pulse is** otherwise quiet, I cure **in** my own simple way, with sugar-coated pills. **To** love, and to marry, **are** two verbs which a young gentleman **of nineteen** years of age generally conjugates incorrectly.

(Again sits down.)

Alas ! this identical first love, although unforgetful through life, **the** idiom **of the soul's** pre-existence—a divine creation, like the petal of a flower, **by which** the botanist recognizes the species—the fullest realization of the ideal of life, its highest spiritual flight, **its most** blissful imagination—how rarely, after all, does **that love sanctify** possession ! Nevertheless, this **first** love, as being **the most priceless** gift from Heaven, shall serve us **as** an undisputed, **therefore an** inestimable dowry to our real happiness, taking **up its** abode within **the** heart, upon **the** sacred threshold **of** which sweet indelible reminiscences **of** the past strew the blue forget-me-not, **in** order to be for **ever revered** as the faithful guardian upon **all our** terrestrial wanderings.

In its **first** awakening, **mirrors** itself the dawn **of** the happiness of life, **directing the heart to find the** paths which lead towards it. **Yet** those paths, upon **which happy youth** makes a confidant of the **gentle** zephyr—oh ! **they are almost** always lost upon **the endless plains of** life. When, at **the hand of Time,** the sky **becoming overcast, youth** is maturing into manhood, **and** is energetically and untiringly climbing over the rough boulders **of** ambition, then it is in particular the poet, the artist, and the composer of symphonies, to whom those **heavenly** paths, amidst their own storms **of life, remain recognizable** to some extent, accountable for only by **the choice** of their spiritually delightful avocations. Those gentlemen, then, are prepared to **conduct** to the theatre not alone their own, but the deeply-affected hearts of a general fashionable audience, rejuvenating **love** to the civilized world at large from **the very** boards of the stage.

(The Doctor suddenly **stoops down,** and picks up a small piece of gilt-edged **paper,** and reads):

" ON PACHECO

" Wreath'd **with** sweet flowers thousandfold,
Art cozily hid by loving May ;
Playful children do betray thy gold,
And proud antlers of a **stag's array** "—etc., etc.

(Smilingly)—Now it is clear the young lady is in love.

(Rising)—And Edwin, **in all probability,** likewise.

(Upon which the Doctor **moved on, but** had only gone a few steps when he observed two young gentlemen at a distance, adroitly getting over a fence and advancing towards him. The light color of the uniform of the Alumni, with its golden epaullettes glistening in the morning sun, enabled him to at once recognize his son Edwin in **one** of those elastic figures who were making for him at the rate of **2.40. Up to his** safe arrival, the Doctor had got **time** enough to hold the following soliloquy):

It will be the best way to send Edwin traveling next year, after his term at college is over. Another country—another love. The **parental home being too** circumscribed, a young gentleman ought to **go** and see the world in order to become thoroughly acquainted with it, **and be** properly accomplished ;—like the fruit, which, only when ripe, **tastes** delicious and refreshes.

In such a condition, **he** ought to marry, lest **he may fall off the** tree of life priceless and nearly useless, having **become worm-eaten** and picked **by** birds. Very similar to the **eagle, which, in his aerial** flights, **sees nothing** but the earth ; and **to which a lamb, black or** white, before a **palace or a hut,** is but **a lamb :** so man, endowed with **reason, should honorably care** for his family, **with** an all-sacrificing love and devotion, by means **of** his own industrious labor, performed either mentally or manually, according **as individual** capacity is developed ; and not **merely labor** for and **protect the** same, but fully comprehend that **the general** solution **of the grand** problem of social life, which **alone exhibits** progress prominently **and is** subordinate to the lawful **rules of civilization,** is found **foremost in marriage.**

EDWIN (approaching, and saluting his father while yet at a distance)—Dear father ! we intended to surprise you, and hoped to find you, surely, in a canoe. We would have swam towards you, that is certain.

DR. GRAEFFE—Pray, my dear son ! this is no lake for you to swim in. Not merely ducks rusticate here, but young ladies take an airing.

EDWIN (abashed)—Dear father ! pray what have you shot?

DR. GRAEFFE—Well, not exactly ducks, and fibs, you know, I don't make ; but a sapphire I have got, which I shall keep, most certainly.

EDWIN (amazed, at the same time changing color)—Oh, father ! you joke, I am sure! Here ! Sapphires?

(Embracing his father, and looking him fondly in the face) :

Alas, father ! do speak ! Tell me all about it. Have the kindness to show me that treasure.

THE DOCTOR (laughing)—Now, that wouldn't be quite advisable yet. For the present, calm yourself, my son ! What is mine, is thine; and a secret is a treasure as well.

ALFRED (who had in the meantime approached, says, suddenly) : Doctor ! we looked for you to ask permission to continue our studies of mineralogy in the vicinity of Martinez.

DR. GRAEFFE (pleased)—Ha, ha ! you are an amateur too ! Why not? California is rich in precious jewels.

(Cordially shaking Alfred by the hand, he added, jocosely)

Your mineralogical cabinet must have become very conspicuously beautiful !

ALFRED (abashed)—Doctor ! I will confess that it is highly attractive to be pleasantly engaged in such a search with friends.

DR. GRAEFFE (nodding):—Isn't it? I am completely convinced of it, my boy; in fact, have been equally enthusiastic while at your age, especially when in really delightful company Besides, it is quite natural, and Edwin has now got the same taste.

ALFRED (gracefully):—Edwin and I have got very similar tastes, which explains our friendship.

THE DOCTOR (shouldering his gun, whispering):—I do declare those are gentlemen. Such men one may as well confide in at once; how hugely their minds have expanded. Man is visibly maturing. Earnestness and dignity, the foremost ornaments of a Chesterfield, are truly theirs.

About to go away, the DOCTOR put his hand into his pocket, drew forth his portmannaie, and cheerfully presented Edwin with **five twenty-dollar pieces—at the** same time shaking both gentlemen by the hand, **saying:—**

Amuse yourselves, and **return** soon and in good health. My dear **Alfred,** present my **compliments** to your parents in Martinez, if you please. Apropos ! how many brothers and sisters have you got?

ALFRED (politely):—My brother Rudolph, who is at present traveling in China, and my sister Bianca.

DR. GRAEFFE, (interested)—Indeed ! Your brother in China? that is novel. Very likely a merchant ?

ALFRED:—I beg your pardon, sir. My brother is studying the language there, which my father thinks has become of very great importance to be made thoroughly acquainted with. My father bases his opinion upon the fact that steam having, so to say, annihilated geographical distances, affords to the civilized world a long desired opportunity of recognizing the barbaric one, in order to prove there, upon the spot, its superiority over the other, by applying its powerful principles of charity on all occasions which the vast commerce of the two countries affords so admirable an opportunity of practicing to mutual advantage.

DR. GRAEFFE:—Certainly a timely idea, and decidedly a far more intelligent one of endeavoring to know the language of a nation of four hundred millions of living people, the commerce of whom is highly important and of direct use to us, than to waste proportionately, precious time upon studying Greek and Latin, in order to fathom the philosophy of defunct nations, by the more than laborious and costly aid of the knowledge of their literature. Besides, the advantages derived from the latter being of a theoretical nature only, are neither practically applicable nor useful to the present enlightened age, except in comparatively isolated instances. As to the heroic deeds of a Cæsarean epoch, they may be a serviceable study for aristocratic Europe, but not for us in free and intelligent America.

We have long ago eschewed feudalism, and learned to care for nothing but the love of God, by the sunshine of a clear conscience, and then directly—for ourselves individually and collectively; by which practicable application of wisdom, strictly within reach of reason and eyesight, we value life and liberty, wealth and health, labor and time, and are twofoldly happy by enjoying life, and remaining ahead of the world, in all reasonable probability, for ever.

Dr. Graeffe (suddenly)—And Miss Bianca?

Alfred—My sister I have brought with me; she shall remain here with Mr. Waldsworth, who is a very kind gentleman, and a great friend of my father.

The Doctor (softly, and with a lovely rebuke)—And you have not got her introduced to us!

Alfred (abashed)—It appears her friend, Miss Tecla, has taken possession of her altogether.

The Doctor (much interested)—And, pray, who is Miss Tecla?

Alfred (frankly)—Her parents reside in Grass Valley; her name is Mallwitz. (Continues, elated)—Dear sir, Miss Tecla plays superbly on the piano!

The Doctor (continues, likewise highly pleased)—Does she, indeed? Why, that is important, to be sure.

Alfred (delighted)—I assure you, dear sir, Miss Tecla possesses a talent so very conspicuous, that there is at Schubert's music-store, in Clay street, nothing sufficiently difficult for her to overcome. She has even astonished Professor Hartmann, who frankly declares, that after her studies shall have been completed, she may well rival in celebrity the two accomplished Misses Laemlein. Already she excels in her execution all the gifted scholars at Waldsworth, and various professors—for instance, Messrs. Holstein, Seib, and Delventhal—are deeply impressed with the wonderful richness of her performance and the precocity of her talent.

The Doctor (softly and friendly)—My dear Alfred, you will promise me one thing—that you and your dear sister, as well as her friend Miss Tecla, will pay us a visit as soon as possible, and as often as you may be pleased to do so. Mrs. Graeffe will likewise be happy to make your acquaintance. As to Mr. and Mrs. Waldsworth, they will no doubt approve of it. Of course, I shall personally endeavor to conquer from those friends the necessary permission, for form's sake. It is doubly pleasing to me that the young ladies are so well cared for. And in regard to the aforementioned professors of music, they are well known as being highly competent to fully develope the brilliant talents of the young ladies.

Alfred—Dear sir, I cannot refrain from thanking you, in the name of all of us; and joyfully assure you, that we shall very much appreciate the honor of being permitted to visit your home.

EDWIN (a little impatient)—Oh, **father**! now do permit us to **call at Mr.** Waldsworth's, **and** request that gentleman to telegraph at once, that we be authorized to take the ladies with us.

THE DOCTOR (quickly)—Above all, have the young ladies consented to go?

ALFRED—Oh, Doctor! we shall beg **very hard.**

DR. GRAEFFE—Well, **then**, do hurry; **it is** already nine o'clock. The carriage I shall have attended to. John shall drive.

EDWIN AND ALFRED (joyfully)—A thousand thanks! We shall be quick—**so very quick!**

EDWIN (suddenly)—**Father**! allow me to carry your gun.

DR. GRAEFFE (while handing him the **gun**, the powder-flask and shot-pouch, laughingly)—**The** caps I shall keep. A **passion** to hunt might disquiet you.

EDWIN AND ALFRED (saluting the Doctor, **walk** quietly away, saying)—Good-bye!

DR. GRAEFFE (looking after them)—Ah! happy love! charming spring of **life**! Oh, may its dream last through it! The deeper the soul is inflamed, the longer the time ere the fire of love is extinguished. Its all-consuming element destroys the allurements of a fast life, conducting youth safely over the dangerous, badly-matched cliffs of unknown shores, leading towards his future **thorough happiness**; enabling him, in due course of time, to prove himself to be a man by the **strength of his fortitude, which he may be** called upon to display **while suffering from the** disappointment of the realization of his earliest, fondest, and dearest hopes.

In this love, which has first germinated from the care of worthy and loving parents, rests securely the great power of morality; its ideal fondly embraces the almighty Creator, in child-like innocence—the world, with joyful looks and generous confidence. Invigorated by hope, it never dies—is eternal as the soul itself.

Yes, that's it! I shall afford him every reasonable opportunity of finding with his Bianca a heaven upon earth. Sure of her love, he will not grieve so much at parting next year. Stimulating his honor, as that love **does**, to carve out for himself an honorable career, that image impressed **upon** his heart may indeed prove a great instrumentality by which he will **be** powerfully **assisted** in attaining to and reaching a probably great eminence in life; at the same time preventing him from listening to what is **vicious** and bad, and wasting his leisure hours upon what is useless and frivolous.

Woe to those parents who endeavor to suffocate and destroy the first, this heaven-inspired love in their children, by bartering heaven to earth with purely worldly stakes of interest—thus exposing the true and lasting happiness of their own children to the dire, abject poverty of their souls, through all the future of their lives.

Above all, I must consult my wife. Her look is sharp—she will be particular in knowing Bianca.

(Suddenly)—Certainly, it is all right ! They must all come to my house before they can leave for Martinez. (Walks off.)

(The curtain falls.)

2

THE SECOND ACT.

(The same scenery as before, **during** the first **act.**)—You suddenly listen to loud singing in an opposite direction to which the Doctor had departed and are not disappointed in finding four students promenading arm in arm singing:

> Gaudiamus igitur
> Juvenesdum sumus
> **Habitare** fratres,
> **Fratres** in unum,
> **Unum** et jucundum,
> **Unum** et jucundum.

The gentlemen having at last arrived upon the same spot as mentioned before, disperse around the same and rejoice vociferously, in ecstatic admiration of the magnificent panorama which presents itself to their views upon which says—

WEBSTER—I should very much like to know where Graeffe **is**!

CLAY—Hav'nt you heard? He shall continue his studies at Berlin!

SUMNER—Likewise Schoenlein, who is said to have got relatives there.

SCHURZ—As to myself I should prefer studying Bismarck.

CLAY—And I to receive from him the vow of a Republican.

WEBSTER—As I do not only admire his plans for unification, which makes me regard his patriotism, I should but like to impress upon his heart the duty of tolerance; of aiding to lift up the masses to liberty and happiness.

SCHURZ—Especially now as the way to it is apparently made free. In a political atmosphere as at present purified, the old feudal spirit of caste will soon wane amid so abundant a development of the mind, and the **debris** be hurled in true student's manner, as if it were witchcraft, **into** the old ivied ruins of their distenanted castles.

SUMNER—The "soon" I am afraid we have to give a large margin to!

SCHURZ—Merit paves its own way, presented by capability as derived from the divine mind, and duly brought forth, expanded and **offered** to sight by the aid of free and **good** schools; it is **ever** correctly weighed by justice, which, like the Creator, never **slights** anything, not **even** a worm.

SUMNER—But who is it that exercises justice in monarchies? Pray, is it man or the aristocrat? Do you intend blaspheming the Creator? rank an aristocrat among His creations?—the idea! Whenever you shall have detected, by aid of your telescope, the stars upon his breast reflecting meteor-like within the milky way upon the canopy of heaven and the broad daylight, arousing all creation to life shall have shown him to you unembossed by patronage and power; valued by merit only, placed by merit only and paid by merit only, thus personally aiding to progress and happy within his mind of having done naught but his duty to his best ability, honestly toward God and mankind, then, sir, and then only, after man has found man, mayest thou rest firmly assured of the justice of God dispensing His mercies impartially.

SCHURZ—Germany is moving in that direction.

SUMMER—Sounding the alarm?

CLAY—At least, you'll admit that she has conquered for herself and Europe a long and lasting peace, and will now sow and reap—manufacture and make money.

SUMNER—With the knapsack upon her back, and the sabre dangling at her side.

SCHURZ—An old, superannuated fashion from Paris.

SUMNER—Then you had better introduce the Dolly-Varden.

SCHURZ—In such a manner did Socrates answer Alcibiades.

SUMNER—And by far more impressively did Washington answer General Howe.

SCHURZ—Our international policy is not the foreign policy of monarchical governments.

SUMNER—So much the worse—so much the more deplorable! because it proves, beyond a doubt, that the monarchical form of government as based upon force abroad—and within, prevents the full development of morality among the people, as consequent upon prescribed liberty; besides offending the common sense of a people who have advanced to the right of being styled a civilized nation. The idea that the Government only has got an undisputed right of shielding the country against invasion, and of maintaining order within, implies the presumption of a belief that the people, of whom they themselves form the minority, cannot do it. More than that, it lays bare the utter selfishness of the principle of aristocracy, as arrogating to itself the absorbance of the inalienable rights of man—his industry—his free-will ; in short, is retarding instead of advancing progress. No better proof of this than America : that all civilization is dutifully subordinate to one great truth ; and that is, the lawful respect for personal liberty. We have demonstrated this truth to Europe for the last ninety-six years, quite quietly ; and, at last, have made it quite lively by it.

SCHURZ—I cannot but quote history, which shows the necessity of self-defense and self-preservation.

SUMNER—Bah ! Feudal times !

SCHURZ—Well, then, do take the latest facts.

SUMNER—The power of France over Europe is crushed, which ends the feudal times ; besides, has at last succeeded in convincing the world of the impossibility of settling-difficulties of any kind by the aid of murderous shot, without either shocking the civilized world, or drawing forth, in all its force, the revenge of the barbaric one, as consequent upon the exercise and indulgence of fury. If that was not an admitted fact, the mythological Mars would be again considered infallible ; the people, thus oppressed, continue to live and die in abject poverty ; and the republic, the only guarantee of the social happiness of a civilized nation, be again suspended for an indefinite length of time.

Inasmuch, however, as we do not strictly value republics only as civilized nations, although we never sympathize with monarchical forms of government, as for ever abjured in 1776, we are nevertheless bound by the principles of charity which pervade our institutions, to interest ourselves at all times in the welfare of mankind ; never despairing to see the remotest cannibal redeemed to civilization. Of course, we do not interfere politically abroad ; because we do not presume to follow the fashion of operating upon the reason of man after his soul has already fled to heaven in the tug of wars. All we can do is to exercise our moral influence upon civilized nations as to disarmament, and to make it obvious to all the world, by the constant prosperity of our own republic, that it is the only form of government, in a civilized age, which guarantees peace as an invulnerable shield to the liberty of man.

CLAY—The mind which applies steam so intelligently, and has learned to interpret nature more wisely than before, is not only developed much stronger to day, but paves the way for its own happiness and that of all mankind much more certainly than was accomplished in the past ; which makes it reasonably sure that man, with such a genius, shall at least understand how to succeed lawfully in freeing himself from oppression all over the civilized world.

Sumner—**Listen, Clay !** If you commence to talk of **the myth of** the commencement of the world's progress in refinement, and are at the same time aware that Europe maintains to-day, by the sweat **of its** brow, about five millions of soldiers ready **to do battle,** fully with-- drawn from the peaceful pursuits of labor, I am afraid it will re- quire many years before it is in the power of the people there to set man at liberty, and to guarantee his happiness.

Schurz—A new era dates from the time **of the** last war, in which **Bismarck has** dissolved the balance of power **as** wielded through **the** principles **of the** monarchical form of government, **and** bril- liantly and **strongly** coated over with the **varnish** of hereditary aris- tocracy—with the powerful spiritual essence of a general **and** compe- tent education.

Sumner—The form is **changed,** but the substance **is not dissolved,** by any means.

Clay— **By-and-by** [quotes **Liebig**] "The principle of republic- anism being **charity,** the exercise of which constitutes the nobility of **the** soul, it becomes evident **that such** an intellectual and moral power must not only eventually, **but speedily, succeed in** subjugating what is eminently physical and coercive."

Schurz—Bismarck **allows himself** to **be sternly led by history** while he firmly faces the presence. Historically **he** knows **the** French, and practically he now concentrates free **from** preventives of a serious kind, the whole Germanic race, **as** monarchically domi- neered over **by** distinct dynasties, **in order to** create a numerical strength, **so vast that it must** forever prove a safeguard against the **re-occurrence of wars, by the very** force of circumstances. Such a **state** of things will also prevent France from listening **a** third time **to her** own monarchical adherents, who have twice upset the **republic, and** would **try it a** third time if not foiled as above. **Thus, inten-** tionally or **not,** Bismarck takes **into** hands the cause **of true** humanity, **as** America views it and thereby **is,** of course, furthering Republican- ism, whether **or** not. Possessed of too brilliant a **genius,** it is not **reasonably to be** apprehended that he should **not be aware that public opinion in** all Europe is **now** rising to vigorously attack **the honor of the aristocrat,** and **to** surely conquer **the** strong Achilles **in the heel.**

Sumner—You don't say, **as if** the world **didn't** know **it before.** 'Pon honor, Lieutenant, when the aristocrat **shall** have been cured of hallucination, **as** Schiller **has** it, the "Wahn" shall have plainly recognized himself in mirror, and shall have correctly understood the

great doctrine of **resurrection,** then and then only are you right, is
Achilles conquered in the heel. Up to that time, however, which is
somewhat veiled by future and procrastinated, **by the study** of Punic
wars, and **other** superlative anti-liberal **vices** will **be** do if
you let him, try, saber in hand. to pronounce himself infallible, pro-
claiming by the roar of the cannon that force is reason and reason **a**
farce. (Laughing)—Let us rather sing **as** melodiously as we can,
Yankee **Doodle,** and thank **the** host of **hosts** that **we** live happily in
free America.

(All are singing Yankee **Doodle.**)

Webster—How sacred our oath of 1776.

Clay—**It is an** addendum to religion, in which the soul **recognizes**
the imperishable happiness of life under the vaulted canopy of heaven.

Sumner—**Approaches** all mankind kindly and peaceably, **with one**
hand fraternally sympathizing with the unfortunate and with **the**
other rejoicing at the happiness of **the** fortunate, banishes hate, **re-**
venge and murder, honors the person, **his** merit and his right; **and**
finds **heaven upon** earth **in a clear conscience.**

Webster—

> Honors the fair sex, fondles the child,
> Guardest sweet joy, blissful so wild,
> May fall not a prey to veil'd future.

Clay—

> Victorious is fidelity,
> Sacrifice o' love's sincerity,
> In each triumph of the rising sun
> Sorrow shall wane which we have begun.

Schurz—

> What would remain of civilization?
> Of the spirit of the times, progress of a nation?
> Naught but to cover well an animated mass
> Of body perishable in its tenement of glass;
> For that life's breath does lift you at each step anew
> That thou mayst see a heaven's love renew.

Sumner—

> It's our purpose thus to please the Deity,
> That from under archways high in liberty,
> We honor friendship for His sake

Webster—

> Continue unabatingly to educate.

Clay—

> To steadily ennoble.

Webster—Did one so appeal feelingly **and** directly to the courage
and dignity of the world, it would bring about a second grand **migra-**
tion of peoples **in** spite of all Bismarckian policies.

SCHURZ—

> Who inherit there the German name?
> Shall heir be to the Hindoo's train,
> And convert him, the cannibal forlorn,
> By the one word "truth" that he is born.

Earthquakes and science having divided the earth into five distinct parts, whom should spring find there to salute?

WEBSTER—We had better salute our spring by migration to Tubbs' Hotel. What do you think?

> (All are singing)
> "Edite, bebite collegiales,
> Post multa secula pocula nulla."

SUMNER—Good! and the Grand Central Park being close by, we have at once one of the most handsome retreats in this earthly paradise!

CLAY—And the earth being round, we may as well afterwards continue on to Temescal, where at Gataneo's, the friend of Garibaldi, we can study astronomy and gastronomy in a highly satisfactory manner.

SCHURZ—Friends! how charming is friendship! how ennobling true tolerance! Like flowers upon the meadow or mountain top, should man meet man, peaceably; and like flowers in a well-cultivated garden should civilized people greet and befriend each other with true brotherly affection.

CLAY—The most charming of all forms of creation are the ladies.

WEBSTER—Beyond a doubt! Comparable only to the sun, with its revivifying warmth.

CLAY—You are in love, Webster!

SCHURZ—You are in hopes, Webster! Hope, sister of presence, conducts happiness safely through the garden walks of civilization into the bowery of nuptial bliss.

SUMNER—Even if storms prevail, the garden walks remain, and you—

CLAY—Friend! we are, happily, too young to know anything of sorrow, and too careless to desire its acquaintance.

WEBSTER—Friends! I shall rely upon my own luck—love, and sleep soundly in the arms of Morpheus until the daybreak of my predestined happiness.

A VOICE (from behind the tree)—"A faint heart never won fair lady" from Providence yet, Agassiz!

(All four friends disappear instantly in the direction of that voice from behind a densely-leaved willow tree.)

(*End of the Second Act.*)

THIRD ACT.

A drawing-room at the house of the Hon'ble Senator Schoenlein, in Martinez. Mrs. Senator Schoenlein, reclining in an arm chair, and using sal-volatile, pensively :

Bianca, I think, will accept him ; indeed, she ought to say, Yes. The chances with Edwin are too risky ; it'll take altogether too long a time before he is in a position to support a wife. Does'nt even write regularly—at least, not during the last eighteen months. Besides, he remains in Europe too long to please me much.

On the other side, Bianca ! years fleet fast and past. One summer chases another, until it is autumn by way of a change. She is like a rose in full bloom, with its odor sweetest—but so only in a garden ; it graces no heart, adorns no bouquet, delighting no one but the passer-by, and even him accidentally ; it is, in fact, at the mercy, more or less tenderly, of the gardener, attracting no especial attention except from humming-birds and butterflies. I, as a mother who dearly loves her child, should prevent my rose from wasting her sweetness on the desert air, especially in California, where there is no excuse for any one not being led to the hymeneal altar.

As to their respective characters, it is my opinion they do not harmonize at all together. Bianca is all life, and very fond of society ; Edwin, sentimental and calm, bordering upon dullness. While, if I take our new visitor, Mr. Lucky, I must say, he appears altogether more suitable. Although neither very handsome nor remarkably entertaining, neither young nor sprightly, he is at least equally elegant and genteel. Besides, and above all other accessory qualifications, he is a marrying man—for the moment, rich ; it is probable he will remain so.

" Nil desperandum !" he will say in Latin, and in English "Never despair !" and he is right. The idea, though, that he avers he loves Bianca, after having seen her but once, is somewhat eccentrical, at least funny ; although quite enough to awaken a lively interest in Bianca, and to astonish me ;—as if I didn't know better than that an experienced gentleman of his standing should not have harbored the sweet sentiment of love in his dear heart before ! Who his first love may have been, of course, remains veiled by the past. It is of no use for me to try to find it out. Upon being remonstrated with, he would very politely say, "Gone !" and sigh deeply—and I be as wise as I ever was.

(Using sal-volatile)—Oh, what *shall* I do ? **It concerns my child**— her happiness through life is at stake. Well off—rich, in fact, as we **are**, Bianca might wait any length of time, as far **as that goes, and** speculate upon 'Change, according to fashion ; **Schoenlein, however,**— rejects the idea flatly, by saying that one **wants a partner for a large** enterprise at once. It **may** be so, after all, for what I know. **Any- how**, Bianca is bent upon residing in San **Francisco. She is the ob- served of all observers—she is a belle ; and her bills at the White** House—in fact, all over Kearny and Montgomery streets, prove it quite lucidly ; and that is all right. The opera **is her bijou, and the** **opera-glass a** companion which she does not permit to leave her **a** **minute.**

(Suddenly rising, **and ringing a** little silver **bell, Mrs. Senator** Schoenlein continued)—I **have made up my** mind.

JULIA enters (knocking)—**Madam, what do you wish ?**

MRS. SENATOR SCHOENLEIN—Be pleased to tell Miss Bianca that I wish to see her.

JULIA (exit)—

Mrs. Senator Schoenlein stepping to the bureau, opens it and takes from it **an** *etui* and a letter, which latter she peruses.

Bianca, softly **entering, approaches her** mother like **a will o' the wisp, and says** affectionately:

Dear mother, what do you desire?

MRS. SENATOR SCHOENLEIN (seriously)—Child, neither do I command you, nor do **I beg** of you to **accept those** diamonds, but to simply esti- mate the value which the *gift* has got for you.

BIANCA (in ecstacy, ejaculating)—My dear, own mother, is Lucky the gallant one ?

Mrs. Senator Schoenlein (touched to the quick) looks at her in astonishment; but Bianca does not give her time to answer, continuing:

Believe me, dear mother, diamonds are **worth a great deal to all** people, including myself.

MRS. SENATOR SCHOENLEIN (seriously)—Are you speaking from your heart, and have you seriously reflected upon what you have just said!

BIANCA—What heart could remain calm at this moment, and what lady find time to reflect much ?

MRS. SENATOR SCHOENLEIN—Listen to me Bianca, you had better cease to think dolefully of Edwin, **and** begin to act sensibly, by substitut-

3

ing Mr. Lucky for him, then you may commence at once to rise conspicuously upon the horizon of fashion. Here, please read this letter.

Bianca (embracing her mother, and kissing her **foundly) said, after a glance over th•** letter:

Dearest mother! I am convinced that Lucky is not bad—only odd. Edwin is good, but acts strangely because **he** never yet surprised me with diamonds; but this is not at all the point. I'll tell you what vexes me. Think of it! he prefers traveling among the Alps of Switzerland with scions of **the** British nobility, instead of with me on **Lake Tahoe.**

Mrs. Senator Schoenlein—I see you are a wife born **for a broker; to-day** rich, **to-morrow poor.** If your husband fails in business, yo u **fail too.** What are the **odds?** But should you, in such a dilemma, be **deprived of** his love. and entirely through **his** own weakness, then **come your trials, although an all-wise** Providence **and** your future **remain to you.**

Bianca—Father has made ample **inquiries. The acquaintances of** Mr. Lucky, and his credit **are** excellent, his wealth in stocks large, **in** fact there is nothing that I know, which might be viewed as an objection. His life is the exchange, and in **the** afternoon the Cliff House, where he enjoys himself in a forlorn **manner, by** watching the dash of **the surf,** and the huge sea lions **tumbling off the** rocks into the briny **deep. Evenings he plays** chess, **at which** scientific game father says **he is very skillful, and** which **proves incontestibly that he** is accustomed **to think clearly and** deeply; also **does he read much, and** good authors only, **being of** opinion that a person who **writes an entertaining** book guarantees **to one,** by what he therein relates, **a pleas**ant evening. Ma, **for that he is a** bachelor **and** ought to **be excused; shouldn't he?** I think I **can** love that man, and **he** too **is so quick about it.**

Mrs. Senator Schoenlein—**Prizes** and **blanks. So** with marriage. **Life** is influenced manifoldly. For instance, **what** we call future **this side of demise, is** nothing more than **our** sensible acting during the presence of life after it has duly arrived. **In** the past of yesterday you didn't know the declaration of **love and** marriage of to-day, **as** accompanied by **a** gift **which** does **not** reasonably permit you to **doubt its** sincerity. Exactly so with **sorrow.** What interests Mr. **Lucky in you so much that, in** case you **should marry him,** you ought **to endeavor to preserve for** him, and **you will have no** sorrows to **lament, because, quite simply** you do **not afford his love an** opportu**nity of diminishing in rapture, and** as **long as man himself does not** sink in his own estimation of a gentleman, you may firmly rely upon him, that he loves as devotedly, sacrificingly and truly, as the lady does whose duty as a wife it is to confide in her husband.

BIANCA. Dearest mother, I pretty nearly comprehend what you say. The presence everything—the future nothing at all besides simply the presence absorbs all my time. As Lucky assures me upon his word of honor that he loves me, and says he would be altogether inconsolable if I did not love him in return, moreover, accompanies his flattering sentiments in so tangible and binding a manner I think, honor bright, that I am in duty bound to accept his love and feel so really. As to Edwin he talks love beautifully in phrases, there is no doubt of it, accompanied by allegorical pictures made very enticing, but does not accompany his assurances either by himself personally, or by souvenirs of a riveting kind, so that I do prefer those set diamonds to the New Mexican ones as inconvertible into substantial love or pocket money either.

MRS. SENATOR SCHOENLEIN—Settled, and right. You marry Mr. Lucky, don't you ?

BIANCA—Yes, dear mother, with your and father's permission.

Suddenly embracing her mother, and nestling her beautiful little head upon her heart she sighs:

Oh! mother! I cannot leave you.

MRS. SENATOR SCHOENLEIN—My child, don't.

Bianca, kissing the mother passionately, appears suddenly quite shocked, saying:

Oh! mother! shall I tell you something ? this Mr. Lucky uses tobacco.

MRS. SENATOR SCHOENLEIN.—Bianca ! I beg of you, don't be childish, and make yourself ridiculous at this moment. Did you ever ! Tobacco ! Why, do you suppose man is a Bactrian camel, that traverses the desert ? The use of tobacco—all you have to do is to wean him from it. You may well console yourself that Mr. Lucky lives generally genteelly, which his appearance best guarantees. As long as a gentleman does not appear in public with decay upon his visage and in his wardrobe, the world is always charitable enough to think that he is getting along in it the best way he can. Of small vices, everybody has got one or more. Whatever the civilization of the age has legitimately introduced to be partaken of, is there for universal benefit, and to be used in a moderate manner, as a matter of course.

No more can a person exist on bread and water only, than he can on love. Ours is a free and rich country, in which everybody does as he likes, and sound sense surely gets the better of wisdom.

AUNT GÜTIG (stepping into the room)—And I tell you, Bianca, never forget that this is a free country, where women have their rights as well as men ; and that, whether head or hand work, we require but one thing, and that is, that every one converts personally the little he knows into money.

The land of ancestry we have left behind, of yore. We ennoble ourselves, and don't allow any one else to do it for us. Proofs endless of this are exhibited in our universal affluence and happiness. All civilization emanates from gentility, and gentility from refinement ; so it is the inward, decorous-feeling of delicacy, with which we think and act, that leads to happiness. Therefore the feeling of charity, which is refinement practiced in life, and without which gentility is incomplete, pervades all civilization, and is the pivot of our glorious institutions. Remark, it costs nothing to be good ; furthermore, that civilization has but one aim, which is, to make every one so good. The gift of life is heavenly and free. To be thoroughly charitable, decorous, and genteel, is to rejoice at the happiness, the luck, the wealth of others, without being envious ; as well as to voluntarily commiserate with the poor and needy, by word and deed. It is liberty republicanized, personal freedom publicly and privately applied.

In this manner, you select your own friends by your own choice ; and so others have got the same rights and privileges. Everybody to his taste. The happiness of one is subordinate to the happiness of all whom the American flag covers ; in fact, the principle includes all mankind, as redeemable to civilivation, for ages to come. Our oath is eternal ; there is no renegading from it, lest the unhappy individual be afflicted with an unsound mind.

Our progress, therefore, is constant, universal, and indissoluble, like the Union which guarantees the very permanency of its blessings to us ; while, at the same time, it encourages the civilized world at large to follow our example, in order to fulfill its destiny.

So be pleased, Bianca, to observe, that charity is the nucleus of all civilization. Your marriage is a charitable act. The marriage of every one—for instance, your maid servant, the poor emigrant who came here to serve you in order to save her earnings, to do what ? to marry—for which she is born ; and whose children may some day occupy higher positions than, possibly, your own.

My dear Bianca, that is what we understand by the universal Yankee nation ; personified independence, leading to individual happiness and collective liberty, to be enjoyed for ever.

(Julia enters slowly, and hands a visiting-card to **Mrs. Senator Schoenlein.**)

MRS. SENATOR SCHOENLEIN (with one look **upon the card**)—Oh, Julia ! be quick ! **conduct** the gentleman here.

Do you, Bianca ! remain here.

(**Hurrying towards the** door, opening it **widely, she almost immediately observed** Mr. **Lucky.**)

Oh, my dearest friend ! a hearty welcome ! I am so glad to see you !

(Offering her hand **to him, she said**):

Pray be seated—here, **near me, if you** please.

(Pointing to an arm-chair.)

And now, my dear friend, **please tell me all about it—the excitement at** the Exchange, to **which you refer in** your **letter, you know, in re-**gard to the newly-discovered diamond field. **Where was it ? I forgot.** New Mexico, wasn't it ? **Is it really so—a fixed fact ?**

HERONIMUS LUCKY (in white vest, elegantly attired *a la* Steil of the Occidental, having taken **a seat** near Mrs. Senator Schoenlein, **said**) —Madam ! there can be **no doubt** any longer ; **the diamonds are** there. The commencement is made. The stock is going **up.**

(Drawing forth a small pocket-book, he **said, as he handed certain papers to the lady**) :

And this **small item—may it please** you, Madam, to accept these shares as a **token of** my sincere regard for yourself and family, and **the earnestness with** which I humbly **trust you** will be pleased to receive my attentions to your daughter

(Bowing, he added)

It is everywhere so viewed, **if we** brokers **present stock we are in** earnest. We try to manifest our sincerity by **it.**

MRS. SENATOR SCHOENLEIN—My dear Lucky ! **Upon the name of Bianca ?**

(Bianca, standing in the bow window, appears greatly agitated—blushes abundantly, **while she looks toward Mr.** Lucky, who is approaching her.)

HERONIMUS LUCKY—My dearest Bianca ! I could not possibly pacify my heart, **which yearned** to strew joy upon your path of life ; so I pictured **you to myself as a** rose, which, before dawn of day, is **beloved and adorned by** dew-drops.

BIANCA (slowly reaching out her hand to Mr. Lucky)—Friend! from my heart, let me thank you; and, as a rose diffuses its sweet odor until it is no more, so long shall I happily remember you.

LUCKY (kissing her hand passionately, quite beside himself)—Oh Bianca! How shall I adequately express my love for you in words?

BIANCA—Love is always meagre of words; rich it is in sweetness and in strength; it is life.

LUCKY (sinks down upon his knees before her)—Then, please take mine.

BIANCA—Rise, Heronimus! Your life I shall deprive you of? shall make me miserable! shall be your death! [throwing herself into his arms.] Every minute I shall count; every kiss put to account, shall make you happy, make you live forever.

While both lovers were keeping books on joint account by double-entry, Senator Schoenlein makes his appearance suddenly.

MRS. SENATOR SCHOENLEIN (observing her husband entering the room, winks lively and on tiptoe, lisps)—Engaged!

BIANCA (recognizing her father, disentwines herself softly from the embrace of Heronimus, and flies toward her father)—Alas, my father! my dear father, how can I ever part from you?

SENATOR SCHOENLEIN—My sweetest child, it is bitter to part from what we love; but it is the course the world takes; how shall it exist otherwise? I bless you. [Kisses Bianca with great fervency.]

MR. LUCKY (having drawn quietly near says)—Pardon me, Senator, that I have trespassed upon form and not first solicited your generous sanction to my marriage with your daughter.

THE SENATOR (shaking Heronimus cordially by the hand)—My dear friend, this sanction I cheerfully grant you, because I hold myself convinced of your love to Bianca, being altogether irresistible [laughingly]. In fact, I can realize your position; Mrs. Schoenlein likewise. Both of us pardon gladly any little discrepancy which a loving heart innocently commits, having to relinquish much which the heart loves most, because in the happiness and welfare of children mirrors itself the contentment of parents.

(Upon which colloquy, Mr. Lucky approaches Mrs. Senator Schoenlein very respectfully, and after having politely and dutifully kissed her hand, says):—

Dearest mother! how shall I ever show myself worthy of so much kindness? express my deep-felt gratitude to you?

Mrs. Senator Schoenlein (reaching out both her hands to Heronimus)—My friend! esteem Bianca, while you love her, and your happiness will be permanent. In that manner Cupid strews his joys forever from his panacopia called Civilization. Mutual attention keeps alive love's constant yearnings. Delicacy and attention assure nuptial bliss through life. The policy you can easily pay ; love is rich, victorious and eternal.

Aunt Gütig—And, my friend, never go to Europe. You absolutely learn nothing there which is good for a philanthropist and republican. If you want to roam, prefer the many charming springs of Eureka, and her lakes and mountain scenery so incomparably lovely ; and if that is not enough for you, go to the Yosemite Valley, or ascend still higher Mounts Shasta, Hood, Whitney or St. Helens, and you have all the Mont Blancs of the Swiss Alps you can possibly need ; always provided Bianca permits you to risk your dear life upon any such elevated adventures.

(Julia enters with a visiting card, which she approaches Mrs. Senator Schoenlein with.)

Mrs. Senator Schoenlein (aloud)—A visit ; a Mr. A. Emsig.

Heronimus Lucky (frightened)—Oh, my friend Emsig, whom I have altogether forgotten at the Hotel.

Mrs. Senator Schoenlein—Julia, please be quick, conduct the gentleman here.

(Mr. Lucky hastening toward the door to meet the gentleman, first says, while Mr. Emsig enters.)

Oh, in my joy I have forgotten you altogether. Pray, do pardon me.

Mr. Emsig (bowing in all directions)—Ladies and Gentlemen, I beg your pardon for this intrusion, I was inconsolable in regard to my friend.

(Bianca advances toward Mr. Emsig.)

Bianca—That is my fault, sir.

Mr. Emsig (bowing)—Then Miss Schoenlein (I suppose I have the honor of addressing Miss Schoenlein) I have every reason to be jealous.

(Mr. Lucky instantaneously introducing Mr. Emsig to the ladies separately and the Senator.)

Mr. Emsig, my most intimate friend.

(Mr. Emsig bows gracefully to each lady and the Senator— Mr. Lucky continuing to introduce.)

And to you, my friend, my bride and her generous parents.

(Mr. Emsig very politely saluting, and beside himself with joy, addresses Heronimus:)

What! you engaged! Alas! friend, let me congratulate you, most cordially so. How I rejoice at your happiness.

(Suddenly serious)—And I! how I feel at this moment that I have made a terrible *faux pas* of not having married. Have you, Heronimus, been hithertofore my only friend, my diversion my second I, so my inanimate wealth, with its superfluous companion "ambition," shall henceforth vex and annoy me. What is Crœsus compared with a Rothschild? and what am I, after all, compared with Crœsus? That is, in a few words, my grief exposed in all its labyrinthian vastness; it lays bare the ominous fact that there is no end to ambition. In the mean time I don't know that I am happy, don't feel that I have every reason to be so; my heart beats so lonely and is so sad.

MR. EMSIG (taking both hands of Heronimus) said—And now tell me once more; tell it me seriously and irrevocably, are you engaged?

HERONIMUS LUCKY (quietly)—Yes, my friend.

MR. EMSIG—Then, my friend, my dear friend, which you are, obey, I beg of you. I shall make you a present of my new house near Lake Merritt, which, by-the-by, is the handsomest of all the palaces which constitute that patrician quarter, as so superbly designed by the original owner of that paradisiacal neighborhood ; and you agree to accept it as a lasting token of my friendship to you, while I go traveling for years to come, and you do not dissuade me from it. In your sanction, rests the sincerity of my friendship.

MR. LUCKY (shaking the hand of Mr. Emsig, says, with great emphasis)—Friend, you are beyond precedent kind and generous ; permit me to thank you a thousand times. As you honor friendship, so I shall honor and love you, next to my Bianca, as the principal guardian of my happiness.

MR. EMSIG (solemnly)—My friend, you are now aware that I have got heart enough to wish you the blessings of Heaven; but you must know that I feel so sad, that I beg of you not to feel offended, if my appearance does not quite correspond with my sentiments. I feel it really too deeply that, with all my wealth, I cannot pacify my heart; being annoyed at having to die intestate. Besides, time presses heavily upon me, as usual, and I must now be back to San Francisco.

Aunt Gütig—Pardon me, sir. Your frankness has quite touched me. If you please, listen to what I shall tell you, and then take due note of it.

Inasmuch as there never was yet a speculation without hope, and just as sure and certain as every one meets with losses in life, so I predict to you that you will lose your heart. Then you shall have found your own happiness fully provided for by the double wealth of contentment and ease, at the cheerful fireside of your own comfortable and sweet home.

Mr. Emsig (bowing)—My dear madame, you will perhaps be pleased to give me credit for politeness, if I do not in the least doubt that you are—upon the subject of terrestrial happiness—the most enlightened and far-seeing lady whom I ever have had the honor of being introduced to, and that I consequently agree with you perfectly as to what would become of me, if I were impecunious to-day. Of course, I would strive to find the wealth of love, and try it for once and forever to base my sole happiness upon it ; but as life appears to me too short now for such a radical state of things generally, and also Cupid, I dare say, has long ago passed in my direction, I fear that it will be but a stray humming-bird, and nothing else, my visits to friends and the club excepted, which shall henceforth enliven and divert me in my lonely hours, when in my conservatory, sipping my coffee, inhaling my Havana, and reading Krause's effusions of love.

Mrs. Senator Schoenlein—Impossible, that in this storm, you can safely return to San Francisco Excuse me, sir ; none of us could possibly permit it.

(The curtain falls.)

Oakland, October 10, 1872.

CONTENTMENT.

—BY—

By Wm. E. F. KRAUSE.

AUTHOR OF SEVERAL ESSAYS IN THE ENGLISH AND GERMAN LANGUAGES.

SAN FRANCISCO:
JOS. WINTERBURN & CO. PRINTERS AND ELECTROTYPERS, 417 CLAY ST.
1885.

CONTENTMENT.

—BY—

By Wm. E. F. KRAUSE.

AUTHOR OF SEVERAL ESSAYS IN THE ENGLISH AND GERMAN LANGUAGES.

SAN FRANCISCO:
JOS. WINTERBURN & CO., PRINTERS AND ELECTROTYPERS, 417 CLAY STREET.
1885.

CONTENTMENT.

PREFACE.

The origin of this pamphlet is a vast parallel which I drew between the light, as during a clear night it is shed by the various planetary objects in space, and by the world-ether is carried to the earth; and the degree of sight, as at the time was left to me, of a cataract of receiving it.

It was indeed a delightful Indian summer night, in which the effulgent light of the larger planets, at the time visible, appearing in bold relief to the surrounding azure, together with a portion of the bevy of asteroids between Mars and Jupiter, and the brilliant fixed stars, as interspersed over the entire canopy, suns of themselves, but appearing like rosettes from their enormous distances, to the Plejades, the center of our sun's and system's cradle—presented a sublime spectacle.

Assuredly, the glittering light of said assemblage, in its magnificent galaxy over a large expanse of the horizon, as embraced by one look, allowed of no comparison of any terrestrial view in sunlight.

But the latter comparison has to be made poetically, because the sight itself of any objects or object, collectively or singly, in the greater depth of space, or upon Earth, is but a sensual delight, and is prosaical because it is real.

Therefore, is it the vastness of the Universe, which the mind is elated at, when it compares the same with the little Earth, as an integral part of it, and which comparison, as the guidance of truth, enables man of finding the entrance to the World, within himself, as the modest abode of his contentment.

The constellations appeared to me, as a matter of course delusively, considering my defective eyesight, brighter than I had ever seen the same. Noticing even the difference in the color, as well as in the size, of the larger planets, as these are visible during a special time of the night, and at certain periods of the year only, besides knowing their several distances from the earth, as computed from the sun of our smaller solar system, I could not refrain, to the great detriment of my fascinating observations, from pondering upon my phenomenal blindness. Not being an oculist, or a specialist of the science of light, I began of paying an earnest attention to the two extremes of my condition, namely: that I could see without glasses of any kind, and almost as instantaneously as reason everywhere in its ethereal sphere travels through complete darkness; the physical light of the planets, all of which being millions of miles away from the earth, except the moon belonging to the earth; and next morning should find myself unable of reading the smaller print of a newspaper, except by the powerful aid of a three-lenses mining-glass. While so my mind was engrossed, a valuable thought passed through its alembic, that, even in total blindness, a man, provided he is at peace with himself, and is shielded against absolute want, can be reconciled to his calamity, and be content with what he cannot alter, and has to endure, as long as he steadfastly bears in mind that he is an integral part of the Universe.

Upon this solid basis I continued to argue the case with myself from a philosophical point of view, and rather quickly came to an anything but pessimistic conclusion, that a blind man, by being saved the trouble of seeing things, which he might just as well have not seen, is in due proportion to his loss of sight, reimbursed by nature with the available compensation that the entire world is shrouded in impenetrable darkness.

INTRODUCTORY.

The object of this pamphlet is to arrive at contentment by reflection upon the Universe, of which the existence of man forms an integral part.

The first step towards it is the constant remembrance of the immensity of the Universe, of which the Earth, as an integral part, is proving to man, by his existence upon it, *the necessity of contentment.*

The second step towards it is, inasmuch as life upon Earth, in plants, animals, and in man, exists within the precincts of their respective independent bodies during a certain period of time only, and then absolutely, untraceably, disappears from the body in death; man, by remembering the Universe, is directed towards realizing *contentment upon earth.*

And the third step towards the attainment to contentment is, the appreciation of the vitally important fact that the ability of man to think, reflect and reason, is available but from one consecutive moment towards another, and in an awake state only; and that, therefore, because of the pressure of time, of practically using his mind: *Time demands contentment.*

THE NECESSITY OF CONTENTMENT.

In my last pamphlet, No. 17. "The World in its Animated Nature," I based the synthetic organization of the world upon the motion of an invisible stuff, called "matter," in its entire volume throughout a boundless space, because said motion or force, upon which the law of gravity depends, could not be obtained unless matter was a stuff, and consequently is of a chemical nature. As such it necessarily is, and by virtue of its spaceless, therefore, incomparable quantity to the world in space, the parent stuff of the visible atoms, which are known to be chemical, and of which the world is made by the aforesaid motion of matter in its entire volume, called "the World-ether."

This is conjectured from the fact **that the** world is arranged in solar systems, consequently, that the atoms so obtained in space from **the** crystals of matter, are there deposited only, called "the cosmical nebulæ," from which a solar system is formed. In æons of time, its accumulated prepondering and solidified igneous mass throws off small parts of its outer bulk into space in portions more or less large, called planets, the by far most ponderous igneous mass **or** sun remaining, but not motionless, because, according to the laws of adhesion and cohesion, established for the Universe, an entire smaller solar system is drawn towards a larger **one, as** is ours towards that of Hercules in the Danaides, by the spaceless and timeless force of the World-ether.

By the same law are governed the fixed stars, which are suns of themselves, and comets in their regular paths around a sun, and all other objects in space. In our solar system Neptune was first thrown into space, then Uranus and the remainder of the planets, and through æons of time of cooling, eventually dissolve in water, and ultimately are absorbed by matter, from whence comes every visible atom, and hence it goes to forever be invisible, as *a stuff.*

With the triumph in physics, **the** gradually increasing development **of** the science of light, the mind is excusably carried away beyond facts, with which science has to deal only. The mind will attempt of knowing what it cannot but conjecture; for instance; what enables the cosmical nebulæ, as composed of the thrown-off, incomparably small particles of matter, and as indivisible atoms are gathered into masses, "molecules," which ultimately form an entire solar system, of becoming an igneous mass?

How could the mere motion of matter in space synthetically organize from said cosmical nebulæ, as necessarily collected in very remote parts of space only, an entire solar system, unless matter was chemical, and as such, is igneous?

That, however, in the progress of ignition, the waterstuff, **as by** far the greater, because finest part of an atom, **must** predominate over the igneous and all other more or less heavier parts of stuff in the same, is easily conjectured, because water extinguishes fire; also, that the fire extinguisher **is able of so** doing. in which latter case it is the cosmical force of the world-ether, which possesses the capability of extinguishing and vice versa in the electric spark is it the producing cause of ignition.

As the earth and moon receive their light from the sun through the carrying capacity **of** the world-ether, so are explained all occurrences within the atmospheric air around this planet, by the cosmical force of the world-ether.

In regard to the position of the earth towards the sun, it for æons of time is much farther away from the sun than when first thrown off the sun into space, because Venus, and still later Mercury had been thrown after it, forcing the earth to farther recede into space, and enabling it at such a distance from the sun in the icy ether of matter of **space of** first cooling at the flattened poles, which accounts for the adaptability of the earth of there having first produced the egg-white of plants, upon which animal bodies develope.

Our earth even proves this systematic process by its fossil remains of animals, at present belonging to the tropics, as having been found in Greenland; also by a wintry chill of atmospheric air, slowly but steadly of late years advancing into the tropics, until in less than two millions of years, the earth, notwithstanding of **being enclosed by** far more water than land, shall be a frozen mass, similar **to** Mars, the only planet of which the glare of the sun allows something definitely of being known.

Of course, the one moon, which accompanies **our** earth, is excepted because it is only 217,000 miles from the earth.

As the southern hemisphere has **got a** much larger volume of water than the northern, botanical and then animal life, became earlier embodied at the south pole than a: the north pole and vicinities, owing to there its heat being tempered by a much larger volume of **water,** surrounding a **much** smaller **body** of land.

8

CONTENTMENT UPON EARTH.

This tenor of the mind is realized by repudiation of every imaginable attempt at a knowledge of what for exists the world.

Not even conjectures are permissible, otherwise than to view the fact of man's existence upon earth from generation to generation, as having advanced upon the preceded ones, and is continuing to advance in more effective moral worth towards himself and fellowmen, until the earth shall have become so cold as to debar the race of man of temporary existence.

It definitely means that neither an exact science nor the idealism of metaphysics can solve this greatest of all problems of what for exists the world, because it is eternally concealed within each invisible crystal of matter of why is it a stuff, and as such is dead; yet when all the crystals are in motion, as eternally they are, said motion, consequent upon each crystal being a stuff, unseen organizes the world, as it is seen. Consequently, it also is the motor of the unseen life of man, as part of its own, within the body, as is the latter seen, or indeed within any other body, whether plant or animal, and duly subjects it to withdrawal from it in death, whether natural or unnatural.

For this palpable reason the entire world can be viewed only as if through a mirror, man being the spectator; take away the mirror, and everything is shrouded in complete darkness, and so remains unrecognizable, except the world within himself, which is brilliantly lit up by Faith, Hope and Charity, and requires no mirror to show him his duties in life, which, if well performed towards fellowmen, are always appreciated as to their intent, if not upon all occasions to his expectations, because of the absolute impossibility of every action being immediately serviceable to everybody.

At the same time common sense tells him that, as he is a world within himself, the outer world—the Universe, with the earth among, upon which his body exists—is not there for nothing. If man cannot com-

prehend what is incomprehensible, he is **not** the less
intelligent, provided that the world's mystery *for* existence is cleared away by himself with the fact *of* its existence.

In order of sustaining such a view of life, it is paramountly necessary that man should add to the prosaical observations upon Earth the poetical reflections upon the Universe, so as to become reconciled to the encasement of his life and mind in a frail body, but at the same time to understand that his mental strength is not to be wasted upon Idealism, only **to** thereby cheer his daily labor.

Neither has man any alternative of thinking otherwise, because he finds upon earth not a single object of Nature, but what is an enigma to him regarding its indispensability of existence. It is there—that is all; consequently is well provided for to exist, in order of playing its part in the household of nature. Their harmony may be established by science, also the adaptedness of their grotesque forms to maintain the body as well as the intricate organism of the body; but why these interesting objects of nature at all exist, and represent Death over the blooming fields of the Earth, that is but entertaining to the man, who lives in the world within himself, and is content?

As indeed the plainest truth always is near at hand, **but** often is searched after in a wrong direction, **so** does the looking-glass prove a brighter light upon the necessity of contentment upon earth, than is shed by the most elaborate understanding of man.

From the cannibal as **a** member of the human race, to the pinnacle of civilization, the morally useful and unselfish man, it is contentment which in both extremes, is the consummation of their actions. To in**duce a** cannibal of discriminating between the nourishment he has to partake of in order of maintaining his body, is, however, less difficult than to traduce the disinterested intent and action of a good man; and why? because the latter feels within his innermost being, what as yet is an undeveloped feeling in the former, that he is for his acts responsible to nobody but himself, and which actions in civilization are amenable to the law of the land only.

It furthermore and conclusively proves that the worth of the human race, as exclusively endowed with self-consciousness, does not lie in their brains, but in their hearts; according to which every woman *can* be in her heart a lady, and every man in his a gentleman.

As to the charms of nature, man may abstract beauty from what he beholds, of especially botanical and zoological, even mineralogical, objects, but he never can comprehend the origin of the necessity for the ferocious instinct of animals, craving food for existence, at the expense of the living bodies of others, as well as the deceptive loveliness of many beautiful and odoriferous flowers, which, together with many herbs, shrubs, etc., also minerals, are poisonous—to one or more races of animals, and not to others.

Upon this swampy ground, swarming with flying insects, without which scavengers of vegetable decay, the entire zoology could not exist, man has to defend himself against it by the devices of his superior mind. Yet in his aborigine state, is inferior to it of viciousness in physical strength only. Pursuant of the law of nature for the human race first was planned an absolute despotism of collectively training human beings, until age after age, through thousands of years of historical lessons in the management of monarchies and republics abroad—George Washington arose and here planted the republic for a collective people, as unhindered by Europe, to individually advance their minds in Freedom, and to unitedly live harmoniously in the United States.

It also has to be borne in mind that the mingled traits of goodness and badness in man, in as much as these are different in every human being and cannot be tempered except by man himself, and also in consideration of the fact that the human race is by nature a social people, are the origin of the republican form of government, where at the present age among a grateful and educated people, man by the moral force of such a natural influence, easily comprehends his duties towards fellow men.

Since steam girdles the earth, and tosses all mankind to and fro, and armaments of war now are so destructive that powerful nations have to prefer arbitration by diplomacy—Republicanism is bound to make steady strides, and the civil law, as the guardian of liberty, be more universally respected, and the Union be revered as the sun of every man's contentment.

That the United States, as the great through-travel of the earth, receives the greatest share of immigration, is self-evident; and although California is geographically situated at the extreme end of the civilized world, yet is its equable and genial climate alone worth the amount of civilization in gold as far east from here as Greece included. It is the most trustworthy guarantee to California of a full settlement of the foothills and valleys, of the long coast and valuable rivers.

Although the population of California of late years shows a marked increase, yet in spite of the advantages above enumerated, is but gradually increasing, may, in an accessory way, be accounted for, namely, by homesickness.

Immigrants, arriving at an age in which the habits of industry, already contracted where they came from, have there taken a firm root, because it is not there, where stood the cradle of man, that he feels at home, but where he has labored during manhood.

Here it is proper to add that whoever understands America, will at once admit that the eternal legacy of George Washington signifies an indissoluble Union, composed of homes, additionally of any years' population of those who come here from foreign lands, able and willing, and law-abidingly to for themselves build up a home, live in it, be happy and content.

TIME DEMANDS CONTENTMENT.

As space and time are forms only of the intellect of man, and do not in reality exist in the objects of nature; whereas the latter visibly appear in space and time, so is the eternal organization of the world spacelessly and timelessly indirectly in it at work of replacing with good material a bad one, so as to keep the world indestructible.

This incessant labor, therefore, is the characteristic of the world-ether within the world. The Universe at large, with our earth in detail, prove it. The mineral abrases, plants appear from tiny seeds, and the entire zoology is born. The germinating process within the seed of a plant, and the physiological and anatomical organization of all living animals prove that life is not a product, but is the cosmical motion of matter itself, in its absolute independence of the atoms with which said motion called the world ether, organizes the body.

By surrounding each atom, and by amassing a number of them in molecules, the world-ether not only forms but models the body, develops it, and eventually makes it appear upon the surface of the earth as a living object of nature in its respective independent individuality of form, whether botanical or zoological. These forms imperceptibly change in their adaptability for existence with the earth in its cooling-off process, which accounts for the gradually diminishing sizes of trees and strength of animals.

The most delicate process of organization, is the later developed self-consciousness of man. It is unlimited, like is the freedom of the will of man to act, but often is instantaneously lost in the vortex of time through interference of untoward circumstances.

This is proved by man being able at the instigation of an innate power of will — of retracing time. While he cannot see forward into the next minute and never can travel faster through life with his ambitious mind—than time, he however, can see backward almost into his cradle, and quickly gather upon that charming road, sweet flowers of experience, to now embellish his ambitious mind, while he is being tossed forward by time.

To illustrate the timelessness as well as the spacelessness of the power of reason, as suddenly instigated by the innate power of will to act—as indeed upon every other occasion—Man is able, while conversing with another upon a totally different subject of transporting his mind scores of years of time into the past and thousands of miles away from the spot upon which he happens to be, without at all losing the coherency of his speech.

Upon the other hand, the most practically reasoning mind, animated by the power of a determined will. cannot of itself, produce a grain of sand without material, therefore, should it be applied to the concerns of life, and of which the body of man, on account of its excessive frailty demands at any time the principal share of attention.

As next to life the freedom of the will to act is its most valuable treasure, it becomes obvious that its province is not only to maintain the body of man because it contains his life, but by its influence upon the mind with its ability of self-conscious reasoning, is to attain to the greatest possible moral worth of man and his ethical advance towards purity of motives through self-culture. Thinking the truth and having an abundance of moments of time of reflection before uttering it, man cannot do more than to act upon it and be rewarded for it within his innermost being with happiness and vice versa with unhappiness in all circumstances of life.

Man so gains in the full freedom of his mind, in happy as well as most trying circumstances of his career, that ineffable bliss, which no words can adequately express, of contentment with his existence as upon a planet, which no matter of what diminutive dimensions is it, is nevertheless an integral part of the universe.

To resume that, the self-consciousness of man is not available in sleep proves that it is an organization of the world-ether, and is entirely unlike life, which, although it likewise is unavailable in sleep, still proves by the fact of life, as it is demonstrated by the breath, the pulse and the warmth of the body of man—the motionary action of the world-ether in a healthy, sick or dying one as well as that, its cosmical force is absolutely independent of the living body until the latter is dead.

Indeed during sleep man has lost his personal identity, he is virtually dead, because he neither knows anything of himself—his ego, nor that he at all lives. In the sleep of death it is the same want of personal identity, which then is lost permanently. During life as in death, life is immortal because vested in the world-ether, and not in the world as being but its attribute.

The availability of the mind of man to reason in an awake state only, and then but from one consecutive moment towards another, which curtails the use of the time of life, inclusively of an unavailable childhood, and an extremely old age, to scarcely half a century of a morally useful labor to civilization, demands this reasoning in order of proving the necessity of a practical application of the mind to the daily concerns of life. But while so at work, idealism must assist man to be happy. An idealism derived of truth, and what truth is more glaring than the immense number of visible constellations, which surround the earth at all distances in the unfathomable depth of space. Indeed without this living company to escort man to the gate of death, the mind could never maintain its serenity as an indispensable requisite of happiness.

Marriage is a safe guide towards contentment. Millions of men have come to an untimely end because of the want of the disinterested love of a devoted wife. Children and household cares prevent man from falling, and make him an important member of the commonwealth. Even when there are no children born or household cares made unnecessary, it is the loving wife who shields the husband.

Marriage is a palpable truth, it is honor to the dead, honor to the living and honor to posterity; it is morality personified and love glorified. Nothing should prevent it and nothing can, not even death, because it cannot separate two loving beings. As these are very rare occurences, marriage is not interfered with.

As we all have rested under the heart of a beloved mother, and when born, were, because of our helplessness, the first subjects of charity, so marriage leads to a life-long calm reflection upon the duties of charity towards others.

In selecting a bride, a gentleman may congratulate himself upon having correctly understood a lady in her rigid reserve and silence, that she loves him more, than she does her own life. She is, when a wife, a light so brilliant that through the darkest clouds of adversity, upon the stormy sea of life, her unfaltering love will surely guide him to the safe shores of a sweet home. And in the gondola of prosperity, in a calm upon the glassy surface of life's charming lake, in the pure, eternal atmosphere of love, such a married life is happiness personified, until the earth bows to the glorious orb, and home has to be reached to be content.

Character, the government of man of himself, governs by its impartial judgment of what is true and what is false in him, not alone his daily actions—but encourages him of cultivating himself in a life among the people, because he cannot possibly rely upon anybody else of better knowing him, than himself.

All unsolicited advice, and every hearsay, all laid-down maxims not suitable to the age in which man happens to be, and the meaning of the contents of anything that is written—would fleet through the alembic of the mind, and be forever lost in oblivion, if man did not possess the faculty of demanding of himself to reason upon it, and remember it as so much knowledge gained of what is good, and so much experience made of what has to be avoided as bad upon his own recognizance.

Knowledge, after all, is but the mould, as it is formed by the mind, and in which the power of will places the respective material, awaiting man to complete the action. But seldom he acts in concert with his will, and as a matter of course the resolution instantaneously weans. The reason is, he prefers of first making a number of different moulds, ere he in good earnest finishes an action with the first one, which with so much vacillation is doubtful. It is the theory of " bad times," because man does not produce an immediately marketable action, to thereby do his share of making the times good.

Economy is the sincere friend of man through life. Not only the poor, but the rich, are constantly advised by it. With the former, this friend becomes often intimate already later in childhood; while with the latter, not always, but occasionally much later in life. Of course, the advice means indefatigable labor, well-performed during such business hours as do not exhaust the frame of either the mind or the body of man, because what is conducive to health facilitates contentment.

Economy, therefore, is not a Pedagogue that forbids pleasure, like does avarice, yet is the advice of economy always: To earn money and to save it!

Indeed, man must possess himself. A life among the people is the world in which he is expected of acting his part of a moral and progressive usefulness to mutual advantage. As it represents persons in all stations of life, he may from any Antaeus learn something of a morally useful and enlightening nature, without at all intruding upon their time and his own, as required, for action. In an active life among the people man learns to think, reflect, reason, and in conformity with law, to act for himself in freedom. Enjoying free speech, as is it complacently listened to by the forum of public opinion, this liberty teaches man more than anything else, of learning to know himself. In independence so appreciated, man is nowhere happier and contented than here, and especially in California, with a salubrious climate unsurpassed.

www.ingramcontent.com/pod-product-compliance
Lightning Source LLC
Chambersburg PA
CBHW021236260626
47172CB00002B/792